Princess Poppy

PLEASE, PLEASE SAVE THE BEES!

JANEY LOUISE JONES

WITH

Jennie Poh

EDEN COOPER

"Grandpa!" called Princess Poppy. "Is it okay if we pick some yummy strawberries, please? We want to make strawberry ice cream for the summer fair," said Poppy.

"Of course!" smiled Grandpa. "Help yourselves, girls.
But my strawberries aren't so good this year."
"Yeah," said Honey, tasting one. "A bit
small and not so sweet. Why is that?"

"If you ask me," said Grandpa, "it's because there
are fewer bumblebees around these days."

"Grandpa? Why are there fewer . . . ?"

But Grandpa's mobile phone rang,
and he started chatting.
The two friends got on with picking berries.

But they were confused!

"Would you like honey on your toast, Poppy?"
asked Mum at breakfast, next morning.
"Yes, please," squealed Poppy.
"Honey is DELICIOUS!"
"We're lucky to have it," said Mum. "Honeybees
seem to be vanishing as fast as bumblebees."

"Why are honeybees vanishing?" asked Poppy.

Honey

But Mum was distracted by the twins. "Oh Angel,
don't put porridge in Archie's hair, please..."

Poppy's brother and sister were keeping Mum busy, and
she could not explain about honeybees after that.

Why are honeybees vanishing? wondered Poppy.
And how are honeybees different from bumblebees?

After breakfast, Poppy rode on her bike to go
and look after her pony, Twinkletoes. On the
way, she heard Granny Bumble chatting to Lilly
Anne Peach from the Beehive beauty salon.

"Something's got to be done to save the bees,"
said Granny Bumble, standing outside the
Bumble Bee's teashop. "There used to be
millions more. Where are the bees? I really
need honey for my famous honeybuns!"

"And I need my spoonful of honey every day to make me
well and beautiful!" said Lilly Anne Peach.

They sounded as confused as Poppy about the bees!
Why do we need to save them? From what?
thought Poppy. *And where have they gone?*

Near the stables, Princess Poppy bumped
into Farmer Meadowsweet.
"Hello, Poppy," he said.
"Hi, Farmer Meadowsweet. I can't
wait for the summer fair!"

"Me too!" he replied. "I just hope
I have enough tomatoes for
Mrs Meadowsweet's jars of
special tomato sauce."
"I hope so. It's so tasty! I have it
on everything!" said Poppy.
"Yes, well, if we don't see more bumblebees,
the tomatoes will be very poor this year."

And with that, Farmer Meadowsweet
set off to work.

Where are the bumblebees?
This is a proper mystery, decided Poppy.

While Poppy groomed her pony, Twinkletoes, she thought about the bumblebees and honeybees.

"Where are all the bees?"
said Princess Poppy.

"Are they lost?

Are they hiding? Are they ill?

Have they been captured?
What if they are hungry or sad?
That would be terrible!

We must find out what's happened
to the bees!" exclaimed Poppy.
"It's URGENT!" And Twinkletoes
whinnied, nodding his head.

A few hours later, Poppy and Honey were walking through Lavender Valley garden centre, looking for a watering can for Grandpa. Both were feeling curious about the missing bees.

"The grown-ups keep saying things about bees but not answering my questions!" complained Poppy. "Yes, I think we should ask someone who has time to explain everything," said Honey, and Poppy agreed.

Sally Meadowsweet worked there, and the girls
were keen to ask her all their questions.

Sally was very happy to help.
"Come on, girls," the farmer's daughter said. "I will take you on a bee trail."
"Yippee!" cried Poppy and Honey. **"This will be cool!"**

They walked until they came to a field, edged by beautiful jewel-coloured wildflowers.

"See the bees in the flowers?" said Sally. "These big fluffy bumblebees are collecting pollen to spread over the fruit and vegetable crops to make them plentiful."

"Wow," said Honey, staring at the busy bumblebees.

Then they walked along a farm track, fringed by a leafy hedgerow, threaded through with bluebells and rambling roses.

"See these smaller bees at work," Sally continued. "These are honeybees, taking nectar from inside the flowers back to their hives to make honey."

"So bumblebees and honeybees are different?" observed Poppy. "Yes, part of the same family, but they do different jobs," said Sally.

"Why are there fewer bees now? asked Honey,
as they walked through a strawberry field.
"Sometimes bees fall ill or their wings don't
form properly," replied Sally.
"Oh no! That's terrible," said Poppy.

"Yes and unfortunately, strong chemicals are often sprayed onto most fruit and vegetable crops, which are harmful to bees," explained Sally.
"That's a shame," said Honey. "Does your dad do that on his farm?"

"He used to," Sally admitted, "but he's learnt that the old-fashioned farming ways are gentler. And finally," Sally continued, "there are fewer and fewer flowers growing in the countryside and in gardens. Bees need flowers to spread pollen across fruits and vegetables."

"So the main thing is, bees need more flowers?" asked Poppy.

"That's exactly right," said Sally. "If people planted more wildflowers, it would really help. Most of our fruits and vegetables wouldn't exist without bees!"
"I couldn't live without fruits and vegetables!" cried Poppy.
"Same," agreed Honey. "This is SERIOUS!"

Back home, Poppy decided she had to tell everyone how planting more flowers could really rescue the bees!

How can I tell everyone in Honeypot Hill? she asked herself. Poppy thought about posters. *That's a waste of paper.* She thought about emailing everyone. *But I don't have everyone's email address.* She even thought about holding a meeting in the village hall. *People might not come.*

"I need to do something EXCITING to tell EVERYONE at once!" she decided.

"I know what!" cried Poppy, her eyes sparkling. "I will organise a bee march at the summer fair. Everyone from school can dress up as a bee and we can hold banners, saying PLEASE, PLEASE SAVE THE BEES! and PLANT FLOWERS FOR BEES, NOW!"

Poppy quickly phoned Honey to tell her all about her amazing plan.

"Yippee! I've always wanted a bee costume!" said Honey.

Poppy couldn't wait to tell Grandpa.

"That's a brilliant idea," said Grandpa. "I'm so proud of you, darling! You've always been a busy bee!" Princess Poppy couldn't stop smiling.

As she ran to her room to think about her costume, Grandpa called after her. "Don't forget about the **waggle dance**," he said.

Poppy stopped in her tracks. "What's the waggle dance?" she asked, turning back to hear more from Grandpa . . .

The day of the summer fair arrived.
It was sunny and warm, and the air smelt of
roses, lilac and strawberries. Poppy and all
her school friends were dressed as bees!

PLANT
FLOWERS!

SAVE
THE
BEES!

They marched through the meadow with
banners and signs about saving bees.

People took photographs and asked lots of bee questions, which Grandpa answered happily. Sally Meadowsweet gave out bags of wildflower seeds to plant new flowers.

After the bee march, the band started to play.

"Come on, everyone. Time for the waggle dance!" said Poppy.
"South a bit, west a bit, turn your nose, waggle your hips towards the best rose!" sang Poppy, with all her heart.

They waggled just like the bees who return to the hive and dance, showing the other bees where the good nectar flowers are. Everyone had so much fun at the summer fair and the bee march was a success!

After the dance, Grandpa was waiting with strawberry ice cream for Poppy and Honey.

"Bees are so clever!" said Princess Poppy, with a big smile.
"They definitely are," said Grandpa.

"That's why they're un-bee-lievably brilliant!"

GRANDPA'S BEE FACTS

Bees are very important to us for many reasons:

ONE THIRD of the food you eat would probably not be available without the help of bees!

BEES also pollinate the flowers of many plants, which become part of the feed for farm animals.

BEES make honey and honeycomb that are yummy treats!

HONEY is also used in many crafts like making candles and in medicine.

IN THE UNITED KINGDOM, there are about 270 different species of bee, and the two most well-known types are the bumblebees and the honeybees.

THINGS YOU CAN DO TO HELP THE BEES!

PLANT WILDFLOWER SEEDS

Brighten up your garden by planting wildflower seeds to grow food for bees. Even a window box is great for bees!

CREATE SHELTER

Allow a patch of grass to grow long to offer bees shelter from the rain.

PROVIDE WATER

Make water available for bees to drink. It can be as simple as a shallow-edged dish of water with some pebbles to help the bees climb out.

BE KIND

Don't put anything on plants and flowers which might harm bees!

JOIN THE FUN! CAN YOU HELP ME FIND THESE CREATURES INSIDE MY STORYBOOK?

Spot these 4 animals in Grandpa's garden.

 Ladybird

 Hedgehog
(He may be sleeping!)

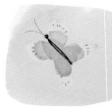 Common Blue Butterfly

 Ant

Search for these 4 creatures in the meadow.

 Harvest Mouse

 Grasshopper

 Lapwing

 Harvestman

Now find these 4 animals in the hedgerow.

 Sparrow

 Badger

 Shield Bug

 Bank Vole